TEJU COLE

PHARMAKON

for Bee, with love

Beyond the circle was a clearing. Beyond the clearing, the forest began. Our group had a plan: when the bus came the next morning, that would be the moment to make a break for it. Some of us would be captured. Some might even be killed. But not all of us could be captured or killed: some would reach the trees, and our plan was made in recognition of that hope.

She was afraid. She went to the Guide, and he told her not to be afraid. Then he prayed for her. The Guide was the man of God; he was the person to talk to when your courage was failing. But I was an atheist—it wasn't my scene.

That night, the Guide drew me aside. He knew the prayers, he said, but he did not know if he believed anymore. I am utterly terrified, he said to me.

When the bus came the next morning, the people were led out of the circle. At no signal, our group made a break for it. At first we ran as a unit, running like people in a dream. Halfway to the pine trees, we fanned out. Then we heard gunshots and began to zigzag. She ran with surprising speed. I saw her dart between a pair of trees to my left. Then she was gone.

I got tangled in barbed wire. The world stopped. My body filled with pain. I remembered an afternoon when I was a little girl, nine years old, the afternoon of my deepest happiness. Swimming in Lake Oso.

My arms were fire, my face was striped with blood. And someone saying, Don't move, you'll only make it worse.

ARCHDUKE

We should go. Give me my coat. Now he will receive us.

You don't know what you're talking about.

No, it's you who's got it wrong. If we go now, he will receive us. Things have changed.

Things have changed, bet. But not for us! You don't know what you're talking about.

Listen. Wait. Listen. Ah. Do you know this. . . lullaby?

Focus, for God's sake. This is no time for music appreciation.

Don't talk to me like that. Give me my coat. We should go. You've seen the reports, he will receive us. What's the worst that could happen?

You. . . comedian. You're not listening. He will receive some, bet. But not us. Have you looked in the mirror lately? Comedian. We are not the ones he will receive. We are the ones he will not receive. The ones he will receive will not be us.

Wait. Ah.

What is it?

Now who's not listening? I told you before. It's the. . . lullaby. It's the. . . sign. Give me my coat. What's the worst that could happen, that he will turn us away? That he will turn us away and we will die? That's all? Then no harm trying.

IN AND OUT OF ROOMS

He is not such a fool as to be unaware that there are certain things one does not say. One does not say, I worked hard and did everything right. Or, I am from a responsible family. And one certainly does not say, It is sad when it happens to ——. But how can it be happening to me?

The problem then is to know what one does say, what one can say. What he says, over and over, to the person next to him is, It's just so strange, it's just so strange.

He has spent his life in and out of rooms. But never has he been in a room like this one, so small on the outside but so large and crowded on the inside. He says to the person next to him, You see, I was given assurances. What is happening to me now is—here he laughs bitterly—so strange.

The person next to him perhaps does not see. A silence settles between them, as though the things that should not have been said have, after all, been said.

Now there goes the ringtone again (it's the "I love you" song), and now they are dragging someone out again.

The concert was free, the pianist's name unfamiliar. There was no printed program. She walked in and sat on the stool and without a word began to play.

For seventy minutes she played, dissolving genres, a sensation of several musics inside one music, a music of pauses and entanglements that learned itself as it flowed forward.

She was a great virtuoso and a child learning to walk, in that chapel where the light was low. There were a dozen people in the audience, a scattered congregation in the shadows.

On my walk home, I was lost several times, as though another walked and not I, and in the months that followed I tried to find the chapel, and failed.

There was no online listing of the concert, no independent evidence of any kind that what had happened had happened. Then I found out, on some classical music blog, that the pianist had died years before.

I spoke to a few people about it in those days, always careful to imply I was confused. But I was not confused. I simply did not wish to be one of those who cannot be trusted with peculiar weather.

THE FATE

Soon we will know if the one to whom we gave the title "king" will choose wisdom or its opposite.

Do you understand nothing? I wear the purple. I sought out the Great Presence as befit my station.

The Great Presence thought otherwise.

I am not to be mocked. My servants visited the terrain and inspected the route and made the arrangements.

Life, O king, is not your plaything. The Great Presence concealed Herself from you. Not all paths welcome a heavy tread.

I am the king.

The Great Presence is not to be summoned by decree.

I am the king.

We made you so.

What is this shit. *I* made me so. *I* give life and take it. I am the king and those responsible for this humiliation have already been punished.

Wait, what is this you say? To your hubris you have added evil?

It is not evil without my say so, and I do not say so.

He never learns. They never learn. (Turning to him.) You never learn. You cannot shout your way into silence, O king. And yet you will be silenced.

Elders! You are old but you are dull. You are fools and you are bores.

Everyone in life faces choices, nothing about that is remarkable.

Banalities, banalities. Already I have plugged my ears to your nonsense.

A drop of ink vanishes on black paper but, on a daybright sheet, it is as full as a moon on a clear night. Were you not king, your folly would be trivial. You are. It isn't. And now the thread unspools.

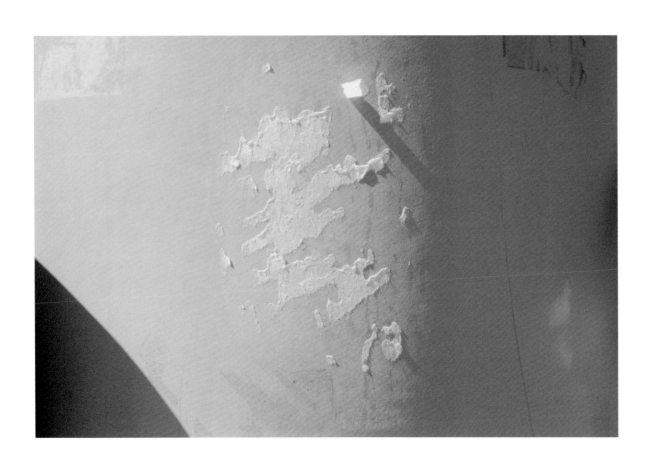

I am writing this note while you're still asleep. It's early enough that I can open the windows in my room. By the time you read this, I'll be at work. Please pardon the strange formality of writing to you when I could just say to you in person what I want to say. But since I have failed to say it, it is reasonable to conclude that I am having some difficulty speaking. Maybe writing will help with the nerves, though I can't see what there is to be nervous about. I am already being digressive. I apologize. It's probably yet another sign of the difficulty of addressing the things on my mind. But even stating that there are "things on my mind" gives the impression that I already know what I want to say, that all I have to do is express myself. That is not the case. There is something I have to say, something I feel it is urgent to say, but I actually do not know, I truly do not know, what it is. So I suppose I am writing this in the hope that the process of writing will lead me to the words I need.

I don't wish to exaggerate, but it seems to me that since you came to be with us something momentous has happened. I'm not sure if what I am describing as "momentous" is more connected to the fact of your arrival or to the fact of your having stayed with us, of your being here with us. Perhaps if you had not stayed, we would not have this sense that things in our lives have changed irrevocably (my husband's life and mine, the life of our son). This is not to say that we in any way wish you had not arrived, or in any way wish you had not stayed. The phrase "changed irrevocably" might convey a negative tone, and that is not my intention. You are here with us now, and you should stay here for as long as seems right to you. We can't decide for you whether you continue to stay with us, or for how long you should stay with us. What we can say is that, for as long as you are here, and for as long as you decide to be here, this house is your house, this home is your home, and none of what I have written should in any way be taken as questioning you, or your arrival, or your having stayed here.

As I said, I am uncertain even of what it is that I wish to say in this already overlong note. I am uncertain of what it is I have to say, and I am conscious of trying your patience by going round in circles. I confess that, in some extremely tired moments, my mind, without evidence, entertains the notion that this situation is less than optimal, the situation of your staying here with us, I mean. Of course, it is a foolish thought, it is an extremely foolish thought, and only in the depth of fatigue could I even conceive such a thought. But is anyone really herself in the depth of fatigue? I cannot trust any of my notions at such moments. Thankfully, I know on a level even deeper than my fatigue that your being here is good. It is the right thing. But even that is the wrong way of saying it, because saying it that way makes it sound as if we were doing something for you, as if we were doing you a favor, when, in reality, it is you who is doing us a favor.

You don't say much, rarely more than a few sentences on any given day, and most of what you say is observational rather than conversational. You might make passing remarks about ants or oncoming rain, but not once have you reminisced about your youth, not once have you asked me about the dictations I sometimes bring home. Occasionally, you make startlingly technical statements. One time, when our air-conditioner cut out, and the temperature inside the house began to rise, I called Icicle and was told that there was a long wait for a repairman. I stepped out of the house, through the back door, and you followed. In the area behind the dining room was the large outdoor unit. It was silent. You looked at it from a distance and smiled. That day was ferociously hot. The turbines in the river had broken down again, and we could smell the bodies.

When we got back inside, I called Icicle one more time. They told me that the repairman had just finished another job and was now on his way to us. It was at that point that you said, That'll be a damaged start capacitor. You offered no further explanation. You turned out to be right, of course—the repairman, when he arrived, used exactly the same words—though it didn't seem appropriate to ask you how you knew. With the exception of such incidents, you hardly speak. You keep your communication minimal, smiling to say yes and smiling to say no. Sometimes you incline your head ever so slightly, and it's unclear whether this indicates yes or no. People who don't know you often assume you're non-verbal.

From the moment you arrived, I had to use my intuition. I suppose that's the word, *intuition*. That first day, I had returned from work about an hour earlier than my husband. Our son was at camp. When you turned up at the door, I was home alone. It took me only a moment to rid myself of the offensive thought that you were *sans papiers*, that you had managed to break free. I invited you in, and the way you walked in and sat down confirmed that you had been expecting to do so. As would later prove to be the norm, the conversation between us was extremely one-sided, me doing almost all the talking. I had the increasing feeling that everything I was telling you was something you already knew. When my husband came in to find us drinking tea, I stood up in haste and said, This is Mirra. I have no idea where the name came from. It just popped into my head. You smiled, and I knew that I had said the right thing, or that what I had said was right enough. That evening, after supper, when I had made your bed and showed you the guest room, again you smiled. I felt in that moment that I was passing a series of tests. That night, as we settled into our bed, my husband and I did not discuss your arrival. We talked instead about what we always talk about: work, the upkeep of the house, plans for our son. The last thing we spoke about before drifting off was the overladen orange trees and what to do about them.

In the days that followed, we carried on with our lives. You were rarely awake when we left in the mornings, but were always there when we returned in the evenings. You were usually sitting in the living room, not occupied with anything, almost as if you were waiting for us to return, though no purpose would be served by implying that you were waiting for us to return. In fact, I see how it could sound insulting to suggest such a thing, and I apologize for putting it that way. You ate supper with us every night. We usually thanked you after the meal for joining us. You never asked for anything. It was for us to anticipate and meet your needs. This was something we learned very quickly. I think we really tried to do our best in this area. More often than not, you ended the night watching a TV series or movie with us. Our son returned from camp later that summer. We introduced you to him and told him that you were staying here now. He seemed confused. Without speaking, he looked at us, his parents, imploringly. (I remember how, when he was born, I swore to protect him with my life.) But he, too, within a few minutes, came to understand. His manner changed; he let go of his hesitation. You smiled.

Above all things, my husband and I wished never to fail you. The months went by, the years. Those of our friends who were able to accept your presence without further explanation remained our friends; the majority could not. I have learned not to judge people for such failures. Our son moved to a different city and we lost touch with him. My husband and I became much older versions of ourselves. We progressed in our careers. My husband was promoted to partner in the law firm that had been retained by the municipality to resolve claims relating to the turbine. We moved to a better house in a better neighborhood. Naturally, you moved with us. Not long after, my husband received his diagnosis.

Sometimes when I open my eyes in the dark, I feel that there is something I have forgotten. What I need to say, what I have been trying to say in this note, is related to this forgetfulness. Now, possibly, I am coming closer to it. Perhaps, finally, I might retrieve it, find the words for it, set it down on paper, and place the paper under your door. Perhaps, finally, the forgotten thing will come back to the surface. But even if I could retrieve it, I cannot be sure of the wisdom in doing so. I do feel I am rambling, so please forgive me. I should probably close the windows now. Perhaps there isn't any question that needs answering, really, or perhaps I have addressed whatever it is already, and this all has more to do with my chaotic thoughts than with you, you who have been with us so steadily all these years. Mirra, I apologize for wasting your time. The main thing is that you should feel at home here, and I think you do. The main thing is that you should feel like our guest. No, not like our guest. Like our host, because it is important to properly recognize who is giving and who is receiving. You have been our host, but even putting it that way does not express clearly enough what it is I am trying to say.

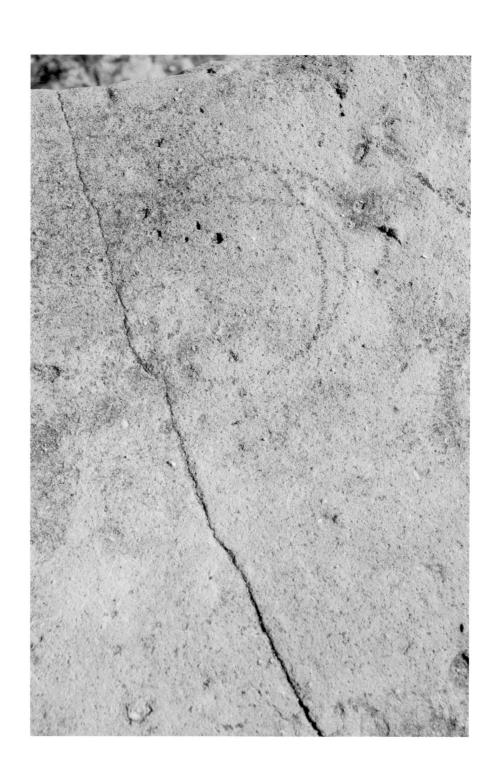

PORTAGE

Asleep in the grass in the dark. Eighty people. The darkness is hot and vast; and ending. Five weeks have passed since departure from Onuino. The place they are going to is far and the way there is hard.

One man is dead, not sleeping. The white man. They have filled him with salt and wrapped him in soft bark. Sorrow in some of them and in some others only forward momentum, the next step, the next.

They are carrying him from the interior to the coast. His too-heavy heart removed and left behind. When he was alive, they served him. Now that he is dead, it is he who serves them. Morning, forward movement. Pastel on the ridges.

Pastel on the far ridges and provisions are running low. It can't be that all seventy-nine of us will reach the coast alive. Now the grass opens its mouths. Now the colors deepen.

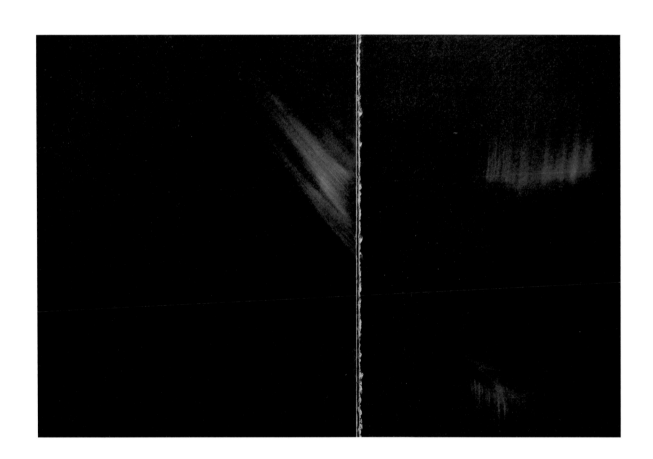

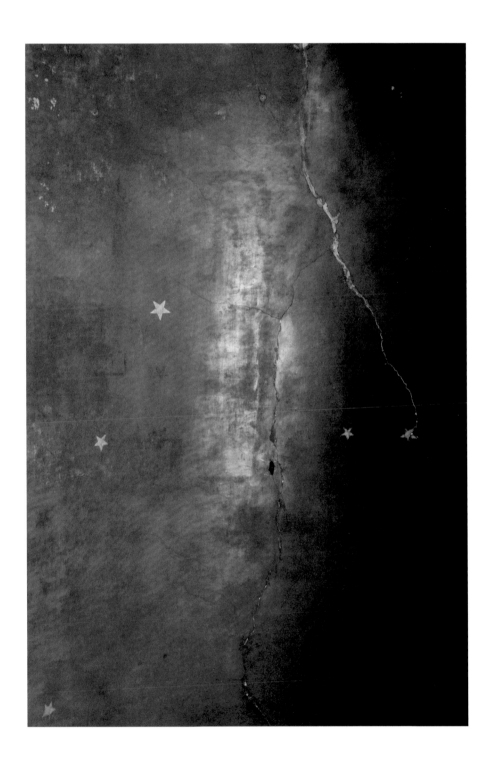

COMPROMISED

The night before everything came to an end, Ms. Prosper finally agreed to sing for us.

She was a serious woman, a small woman with a heavy manner, though some later recalled a twinkle in her eye, and others a dry sense of humor.

I remember only that her presence was full of undescribed life and uncheapened by conclusions.

But, ah, when she began to sing, the seriousness was like oil she had saved for a day of need. The song came out of her light and young, a hint at what she must have been before we knew her. She held the final note of each phrase for a long time.

As we listened to the song that night in the apartment, a song in a dialect with few living speakers, a song she sang with no gesture toward previous fame, the things that were to bring an end to everything were already happening.

We had been compromised.

The next morning, Ms. Prosper and the other leaders were arrested and taken to ——.

Mint goes right to your head. Its leaves are pebbled leather. Thyme is the stubborn memory of wood, with a trace of cloves. Sage has large outstretched gray-green hands. Rosemary is the pine's twin sister.

His route to work is a bus and a transfer to the Red Line and a transfer to the
Green Line, a trip he can make in an hour if there are no delays. There are often
delays. He's not going in today, due to illness. Besides, it is one of the hottest days
on record. He texts her: I'm not coming in, please take care of things. I owe you!
Oh, he adds, don't forget to sign the sheet.

She props the door of the men's bathroom open with her cart. From downstairs
comes the sound of rehearsal. Unsettling, this music. Who died? She cleans the
urinals, the toilet bowls, the sinks, the tiled white floor, and when she's done she
disposes of her gloves. The music brightens and is now nearly triumphant, and
certainly worse.

On each of seven rows he has signed his name—one for each day, each time
joining up the letters. On the eighth row she signs her name, every letter clear
and separate. Above each "i," she places a little circle.

A LETTER ARRIVES

Our pallets are side by side on the concrete floor. I am too cold to sleep, as usual. It must be the middle of the night now, though I can't say for sure, as this place has no windows and the lights are always on. I watch your sleeping hands.

The letter arrived two or three days ago. Neither of us could read it. But word went around that a letter had arrived, and the others murmured. Later we found someone who could read it. The letter was addressed to us, said the one who could read it, no question about that. But it contained nothing about our petition.

Nothing about our petition? I said.
That's right, nothing about your petition.
Must be some kind of mistake, I said. What does it contain?

After a long silence, the one who could read it began to read: Your life well lived. Your life well lived intersects with our institutional priorities and our talent strategy. In these unprecedented times, we are making holistic investments to target these factors.

That can't be right, I said.
Probably some kind of code, you said.
Some kind of code?
Yes. About our petition. We need to find an interpreter.

An interpreter! Where do you think you are? I said.
Wherever it may be, I am not here to be insulted, you said. And anyway, who are you to say what counts and what doesn't count? At least a letter arrived. Not everyone has that.

The one who could read it, ignoring our bickering, went on: Your life well lived can be made operational under four modalities: an active mind, a healthy body, a flourishing workplace, and a sound financial plan. Download the YourLifeWellLived app for more information.

That was yesterday or the day before, it's hard to keep track of time here. Between your pallet and the concrete floor is the letter. Your dear hands twitch as you sleep, seeking warmth alongside your body.

The room in the one-room house was of medium size, which meant the house was small. Outside, it had stopped snowing. But there had been so much snowfall that the roads were impassable, that was for sure. There was little choice but to wait it out.

The room and the two people in it might as well have been a space shuttle and its passengers. A space shuttle would have been nice, but the room wasn't nice. It had two windows, both of which faced out onto a snowy landscape. The white field went a little distance and came to an end at a line of trees.

The room had one door, but that hadn't been opened in a while. The windows, intact, lacked insulation. The room was not warm. The room was cold, but it was not as cold as the woods—for those who like to count blessings.

They sat on plastic chairs. You know the chairs: those white chairs one sees in all the countries of the world, cheap molded chairs each of which is like a large drawing of a tooth. They sat on the chairs, waiting. The room was otherwise bare. They each held a phone which was connected to a battery pack. The battery packs were failing.

The room was bisected by a chalk line drawn perpendicular to the windows. The chairs were on the same side of the line, side by side, about two or three feet apart, facing the other side of the room. There was no coming or going with this snow, that was for sure. Whatever had to happen had to happen here.

Any news?
News about what?
The application forms.
No bars.
Still no bars?
Not out here, so near the woods. And not in this snow, that's for sure.
What has snow to do with it?

They wondered if moving closer to the windows would be the thing to do, and they both looked in that direction.

CIRCLE

You cannot write about the circle from inside the circle. To write about the circle, you have to be outside it.

No, he thinks, that's not quite right: you could write about the circle from inside the circle. It would have to be possible, and perhaps necessary.

In his dry, quiet, warm room, he writes the word into a sentence. In the sentence that follows, he writes the word again.

He returns to the two sentences day after day, for many days. The word "killed" is not quite right. The sentences look painted. But he cannot find another word.

"Killed." Inside the circle, the word it means death, one's own death or the death of another. Outside the circle, it means showtime.

Not that he doesn't know what eventually happened to the one who designed a hollow brass bull that converted the cries of those being roasted inside it into music, their charred flesh into incense, their blackened bones into jewels.

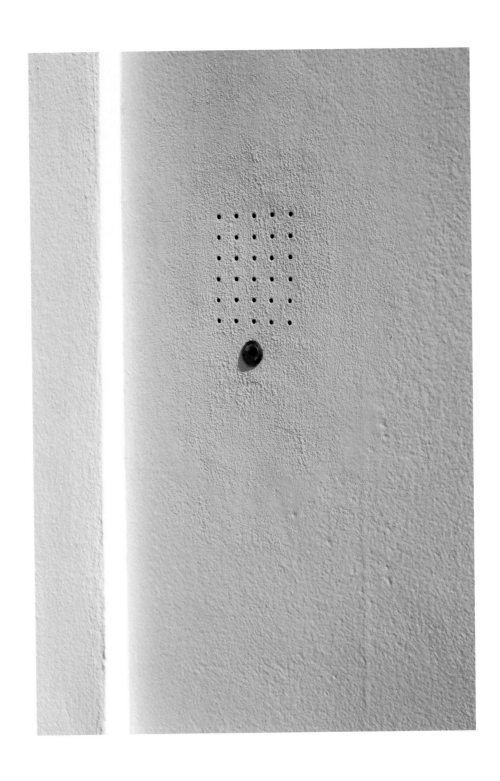

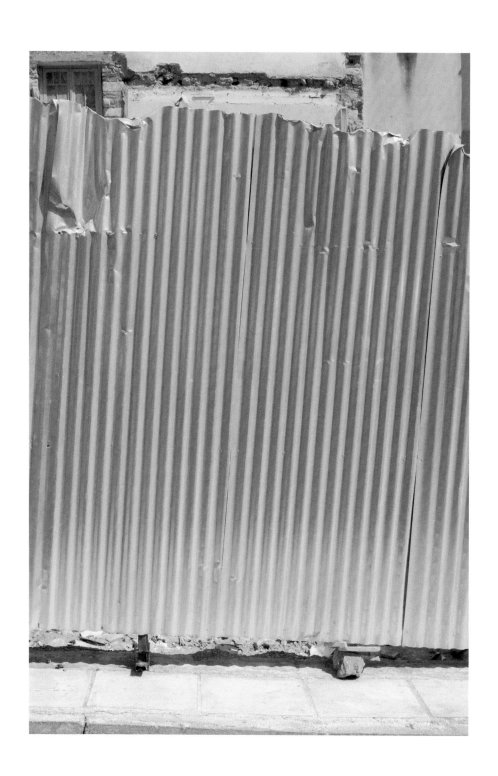